Presley

Parenting on the Spectrum

Andre Reveleno Campbell

ISBN: 978-1-7371285-4-0

DEDICATION

To God be the glory and to my wonderful twin daughters for giving me inspiration each and every day.

CONTENTS

ACKNOWLEDGMENTS

Thank you to my editor Dr. Donna-Neisha Steele.

1 THE BACK-STORY

This is the story of Presley's life from childhood to adulthood and the pride of his whole existence, his daughter. The story is an account of the difficulties faced by Presley as he attempted to live a normal life despite the setback of having lower than average social development issues. Presley fought hard to triumph over his obstacles, but none was more challenging than raising a child. His daughter brought him joy and an overabundance of pride in her early years. However, as she grew, raising her became very difficult for Presley to handle. The joy he knew when she was a child eventually turned to pain and heartbreak as she got older.

-The Beginning-

Presley was a very humble man; some would even call him simple. He didn't have much and didn't have much going for him. Though he was good-looking, his simple, almost innocent persona always made him susceptible to abuse and people taking advantage of him (in this case looks did not help him get by). Born in a home filled with love and support from both parents, it was hard for Presley to understand the harsh world that confronted him daily. The blame for this was squarely on the shoulders of his parents. They coddled him too much as a child, most likely due to social and behavioral deficits; the very reason they kept him out of the public school system and home schooled him for most of his life.

Presley's parents were both from the island nation of Jamaica. They met at a young age and knew they belonged together from then on, so it was no surprise that they got married young. Presley's father, Mr. Goodson, had the opportunity to relocate to the United States. He later had his wife join him once he established a stable life for them both.

Eventually they were both settled and happy, each well-educated, and in a great place professionally. Presley's father worked for a top-notch engineering firm while his mother owned a little boutique store in the heart of the city. When the time came to have children, they struggled for a while trying to have a baby. It wasn't until they went back home to Jamaica for vacation, they succeeded in doing so. They went back to the United States refreshed and ready to pick back up on life. However, not long after, their lives were interrupted by the very best news.

As soon as they found out the baby was to be a boy, his father already knew his name would be Presley. He was such a huge fan of Elvis Presley that he always said he would name his first son after him, and he made true on his promise.

The years passed and Presley enjoyed those years living with his parents. His mother hired a manager to run the shop for her while she stayed at home with Presley. She nurtured him and taught him most of life's lessons. She educated him through a home-schooling program and what she didn't teach him, his father did, mainly technical and mathematical principles. His parents were amazed that he soaked up all they had taught him and was able to retain all the information. They were resolved to know Presley would not be like other kids, but they saw it from a negative point-of-view. Though he was socially inept and seemingly slower than his peers, the truth was, he was much more advanced than most kids his age or even older. Presley simply lacked the capacity to express himself the way "normal" kids would. By the time Presley reached high school age, he knew more than any other child at his age but was still socially awkward. He was technically brilliant beyond his years; almost genius-like, but as fate would have it, he was socially inept. His speech was slow and at times somewhat labored. His posture was slumped, and he always seemed to be looking off into space, as if lost in his own world. His parents constantly worried about him and feared for his future. Both parents agreed that they would keep him out of the school system until he was much older. At the time his parents thought this was the best course of action.

4

Tragedy struck Presley when he lost both of his parents in a car accident. Presley's father, the romantic that he was, planned an elaborate anniversary celebration for his wife and himself. He went all out. First Mr. Goodson arranged for his sister-in-law Ena to take care of Presley while they were out. After saying their goodbyes, they left, not knowing it would be their last time seeing Presley.

Mr. Goodson planned a full day of activities. The spa in the morning, a catered picnic lunch on the beach in the afternoon, followed by a concert by Presley mom's favorite band. After the concert, Mr. Goodson whisked his wife off to a quieter affair in the form of a beautiful romantic dinner at one of the finest restaurants on the outskirts of their little suburban town. The evening was magical but quickly took a turn for the worse. On the drive home the weather became bad and created very hazardous conditions. Torrential rain began to pelt the car with unyielding mercy. Visibility was extremely low, and the road conditions were becoming dangerous by the minute. As Mr. and Mrs. Goodson hit a dangerous blind corner aptly nicknamed Dead Man's Bend, a car coming from the opposite direction lost control and careened into them. The other car hit the driver's side rear corner of Mr. Goodson's car, sending it into an uncontrolled spiral and right over the edge of Dead Man's Bend. As they went over the edge Mr. and Mrs. Goodson linked hands, lovingly gazed into each other's eyes and said "I love you" in unison. In that heart-wrenching moment, just like that, Presley was an orphan.

Never having dealt with grief, Presley was naturally in a new realm and could not contain his emotions when his aunt told him the sad news. He completely shut down and was unresponsive for what seemed like two weeks while in custody of his aunt. Then one day, as quickly as he fell into a catatonic-like state; Presley was re-animated and became his old simple self again.

He was taken in by his aunt who already had two mouths to feed and care for. However, as family she felt compelled to take him in. Aunt Ena was a very kind and loving person, though she was not as well-off financially as her sister. As a single mother she worked extremely hard to give her boys a comfortable life, and now she had one more mouth to feed. As rough as it seemed, she was determined to make sure Presley had a nice, stable environment where he would feel at home. She was very religious and enjoyed the church she attended; the boys joined her every week. Like any other young person, her boys hated getting up on Saturdays to go to church. They would rather sleep in on the weekends, as they had to wake up early every day for school. Nevertheless, Aunt Ena would not have it any other way. Her boys had to know God and going to church was their way of showing him respect. Presley on the other hand did not mind going to church and found that it was a very enjoyable experience. Each visit drew him closer and closer to God that everyone talked about and worshiped. He especially liked the part about praying to God to thank him and ask for help when he needed it most. Presley constantly prayed for his aunt, his cousins, and to be smarter. By no means was Presley stupid or uneducated, but he believed that he was dumb based on his interactions with people outside of his family. People treated him like a simpleton, based on his innocence and demeanor.

Though a teenager, he had the mind of a genius, but the personality of a nine-year-old child. Aunt Ena continued to be a positive influence in Presley's life along with the help of her sons John and Moses. John was the elder of the two boys at 17 years old: a junior in high school and captain of the varsity basketball team. He stood 6 feet 6 inches tall, but with a slim, very gangly frame. Moses, the younger brother was not much of an athlete. He was more into science and engineering. He was one year behind his big brother in high school. His hope was to one day become a rocket scientist. He was fascinated by space shuttles from a very young age and his goal was to one day have his own company that build shuttles. He also wanted to be the first to develop a new type of energy source that was renewable and would not have an adverse effect on the environment. Aunt Ena believed her sons would be great role models for Presley and she made sure that they took care of him, especially at their school.

The passing of Presley's parents brought an end to the era of home-schooling and meant that he had to attend high school with his cousins. This new situation suited Presley very much, as attending school meant a new adventure for him. He was scared but still so excited he could barely contain himself the night before the first day of school. After a very restless night, the sun finally peaked in through the slits of the curtains to illuminate the room Presley shared with his cousin Moses. The bright light of the sun was enough to pry open the eyes of the sleeping boys. Presley immediately sprang into action anticipating the day ahead. All three boys hurried to get ready to catch the bus to school, with the excitement of a child, Presley could not wait for the bus ride to school. Most teenagers would have been embarrassed to be seen with Presley, but with the strong moral codes instilled in them, John and Moses were not like most teens. They were happy to be there with their cousin on the first day, in his new world. They were a good support system for Presley in what was perhaps his most stressful, albeit exciting day. The school was like any other high school in the nation. The different factions of young adults gathered in groups of similar interests and classification. The usual amalgamation of sports jocks, drama and theatre geeks, band geeks, nerds, fashion queens, and pot heads.

Presley was amazed by the stark contrast of the group's mentality and was determined not to be limited to a single clique. He wanted to be friends with everyone and thought that everyone should adopt these same principles. However, high school students can be very mean and did not see Presley as he saw them. The so-called cool kids made sure everyone knew their place and Presley was no different. He immediately was cast aside by many of his classmates for being different, but through it all Presley remained optimistic despite his short-sighted peers. One would have thought that with all the coddling he had as a child he would have a weaker disposition in the face of such harsh treatment. Presley had quite the opposite reaction. He was much tougher than the psychology of his up-bringing would have us believe.

Presley's first and second year of high school came and went in a flash. Those two years were very enjoyable for young Presley. Though small, he had his merry band of friends that he hung with. They all got along well and despite Presley's shortcomings they saw past it, true friends indeed. Presley still tried to interact with others including the so-called cool kids', but they mostly just tolerated him.

School work on the other hand was more gracious to Presley than his fellow compatriots. The first year of school seemed to come natural to him. The work was somewhat a breeze, while others struggled. The so-called nerds quickly caught on to this and eventually embraced him into their fold. Presley was then getting involved with clubs such as the science club, engineering club, and the chess club. His involvement led to several prestigious awards for the school from engineering projects he designed and constructed. The chess club won tournaments throughout the county because of Presley. One of his experiments won notoriety amongst top scholars for its everyday practical use in the reduction of Carbon Dioxide in the atmosphere. Presley was enjoying his first two years of school, but only in his little circle of friends and his teachers. He still struggled to connect with the other kids of his school, though not for lack of trying.

Presley's sophomore year was just as much fun as his freshman year. He was once again involved with all his clubs, and he stuck to his core friends as well as some kids from his activity clubs.

2 LIFE AFTER HIGH SCHOOL

In his last two years of high school Presley's engineering prowess and mechanical genius captured the attention of several technology firms. The one that most appealed to Presley was EnviroTech. It was one of the world's foremost leaders in technology that benefited the environment. It set the trend for most companies in pursuit of environmental excellence. The multi-billion-dollar firm had made the biggest stride in curbing the release of greenhouse gases into the atmosphere and aimed to do even more. The company was also interested in Presley for the machine he had invented in his first year of high school. He made improvements on it in his sophomore year. The machine removed harmful ozone depleting gases and broke them down into less harmful compounds. EnviroTech offered a contract to Presley for his invention and for employment at the firm. Aunt Ena immediately sought the advice of a lawyer to ensure the company did not try to cheat Presley out of his invention. However, the lawyer did not find any flaws in the contract EnviroTech offered to Presley. Presley would be well paid, with great benefits. He would also receive a villa paid for by the company. Presley would indeed be living the good life. However, Aunt Ena quickly pulled him back to reality, drawing on her own experiences. She showed him that anything could happen, and he needed to be prepared. Being prepared meant that Presley had to promise is Aunt he would complete his high school education, then graduate college with a degree. It is the way of West Indian people. If you have the chance and the opportunity to go to college, you better not pass it up. The Caribbean mindset is that you are nothing in this world without a college education. Aunt Ena held strongly to this belief and tried to instill it in Presley. Most people in Presley's situation would brush her aside and live in the moment; taking full advantage of the lifestyle that EnviroTech was offering him. If you knew Presley, then you would know that was not his style. His humble, mild-mannered personality took into consideration what his aunt told him and did just what she advised him to do. After graduating from High School, Presley went to work for EnviroTech with the understanding that he would also complete is college career.

While working at his job with EnviroTech, he attended night classes at his local community college. There he was exposed to the various disciplines of the engineering world from mechanical, electrical, civil, and even chemical engineering. He was fascinated by all of them and applied what he learned in his everyday work life. In no time Presley graduated from his local community college and transitioned to the nearest state university; approximately 10 miles from his home and even closer to his job. Presley did not drive and could not grasp the concept of driving, so he had a driver; yet another perk of working at EnviroTech. They provided Presley with on-call drivers that were available to him whenever he needed. The convenience of having the drivers helped Presley to focus more on other tasks; whether school-related or work-related. In the end Presley completed school in two years. This would have taken the average individual 4 to 5 years between community college and the state university.

Presley experienced a new life changing moment in time. It seemed in his last year of school at the state university; Presley encountered feelings and physical changes within himself far more powerful than he had ever felt before. It always seems to happen in the computer room of the library; every time he interacted with the attending student worker there at the front desk. Her name was Stacy. Carmel colored skin with soft curly hair; she was the very definition of beauty. Her light green eyes with specs of hazel trimming, the outer layer of her pupils was like a highlighted outline, drawing you into the warm glow of her sparkling gaze. In addition, her smile so radiant, incited a riot within Presley's mind. He struggled to find the most perfect thing to say. He needed to engage this perfect creature. Perhaps, start a sentence that leads to a conversation, that leads to a lifetime of conversations, that ultimately leads to a lifetime together. However, first he must find the courage to utter a simple phrase.

"Yes, thank you, computer workstation 4 is just fine,"

Instead of staring blankly at her after her question:

"Is computer workstation 4 okay for you?"

He humbly walked to computer workstation 4. As he did so, he encouraged himself that the next time he came to use the computer lab he would say something to her. However, despite the pep talk to himself, the admiration was just that, admiration. From afar he looked on each day, facing the same dilemma of men everywhere; how to approach a woman he likes? It took months for Presley to get up the nerve to hold the shortest of conversations with Stacy, but for him it was worth it. She was so very nice. At times, Presley wondered if she was being nice out of pity for his condition. In any case he did not care, if in those brief moments he had her undivided attention. Their conversations went from short banter to much more extended conversations over time; sometimes losing track of the time. They found that they both had similar interests and as an aspiring engineer herself, Stacy found that Presley was quite knowledgeable and hoped to learn from him.

Presley did not think that he would have had a shot with Stacy. He saw the relationship for what he thought it was; two colleagues discussing engineering. However, what Presley did not know was that Stacy genuinely cared for him, despite what he has grown to accept as a disability. One day Presley decided to ask Stacy out. Maybe he was inspired that day by something she was wearing, maybe her fragrance, or maybe it was the way her eyes sparkled when she looked at him. Whatever it was, nothing was going to stop him, cue the big hulking man mountain she called a boyfriend. Yep, as he was about to call forth the heavens to get behind him and push him towards this great destiny of finally asking her out, he discovered there was the man in her life. An All-American football player destined for his own glory had already laid claim to the heart of Presley's fair first love. Seeing Presley as no threat her boyfriend simply excused his way in, interrupting their conversation

"Ahh, Stacy we have to go, we're going to be late for our

movie."

Still speechless and utterly shocked, Presley could only look on as they both excused themselves from his presence, leaving him standing there motionless. He eventually managed to gather himself enough to wave goodbye. Feelings of fear and excitement quickly turned into anger. Like most men who were rejected, even if unintentional. He sought refuge in thoughts of inadequacy and self-loathing. He was angry at himself for believing that anyone like her would be interested in someone like him. Still, he was determined not to let this cloud the fact that both Stacy and he spoke well together. He vowed to not let his emotions get in the way of a great friendship. They continued their friendship throughout the year until Presley was ready to graduate. They were to remain friends and stay in touch by phone, maybe even occasional visits. Stacy joked that she was almost out of school and would soon join Presley on the outside as if to hint that college was some sort of prison. On Presley's graduation day they both said their official final farewells. Deep down they both knew once they went their separate ways, life would take over, leading them down separate paths and further away from each other. However, they were contented with the notion that they will "stay in touch".

Now with the confines of school no longer holding him back and an aunt made happy, Presley could freely move on to big and better things. His head was filled with ideas and designs that were clamoring to break free from his mind unto paper. The mundane lessons of his classes in combination with his day-to-day tasks at work proved to be somewhat distracting. These distractions hampered fluid thoughts that he could have formulated into a visual plan, including the best distraction yet, Stacy. He did try to keep up to his promise of staying in touch with Stacy and was successful for a brief period. Eventually life made it harder to do so. Sometimes he would "just miss" her on her land line, or her mobile phone was unresponsive. Other times she was either out with her boyfriend or just too busy with classes to talk. Presley eventually decided to leave things the way they were, as his responsibilities at his job increased with the role of team leader. The calls to Stacy became fewer and fewer, until there were none. That's how Presley wanted to leave it. Now, all his time was spent learning how to cope with the constraints of his new role and adapt to change once again.

Now one might say what kind of company would put someone like Presley in charge of other people. He wouldn't know how to handle other people. On the contrary, dealing with people was one of the qualities which Presley excelled. He has been dealing with all types of people from all walks of life since high school due to his, at times, child-like state. Maybe it was why he excelled at connecting with people. He approached everyone with the eyes and heart of a child; filled with love and kindness. It was as if he had a superpower to turn even the most hardened thug into a true human being. Many times, throughout his life he faced the meanest of people and those that sought to cause him harm. However, the love that he showed to them somehow managed to overwhelm them with a deep inner sadness that brought them together as if they were already old friends. His aunt believed that the love his parents had for each other was so strong and perfect. Presley, being the product of their love, was blessed by God to carry an eternal supply of love within him; forever linking him to his parents. It is the reason his aunt thought his mental state is that of a child, because who loves and approaches the world with such innocence and kindness as a child left uncorrupted. The owner of Presley's company knew this about him and has experienced his power to reach people firsthand. As a matter of fact, the decision to promote Presley was made shortly after he started at the job, but the owner felt that Presley needed to have some experience in the business first.

3 THE REUNION

"Guess who!",

a familiar voice exclaimed. Eyes covered; Presley could only depend on his senses of smell, touch, and hearing. The scent of vanilla hand cream, the tenderness of the hands covering his eyes, and the most important clue of all, tone of voice. This could only be one person.

"Aunt Ena!", Presley shouted,

"What are you doing here?"

She explained that she was so proud of him and wanted to see where he worked. However, knowing his aunt, Presley sensed that there was something else she wanted to tell him. His notion was proven not long after his aunt arrived. She told him that a young lady stopped by her house looking for him and wanted to know if she had a number on which he could be reached. The old number did not work anymore, since Presley changed his cell phone and acquired a new number about two weeks prior. Aunt Ena, not knowing the situation, told the young lady she would check and let her know in a few days. This excuse bought her enough time to talk to Presley first. Aunt Ena continued to inform Presley that the young lady left her contact information and left. Presley knew who it was before his aunt could give him the information. Stacy!? She was back. Presley was surprised indeed. His emotions were all over the place. It was a bittersweet moment for him. He would love to see her, but he was afraid of having the same feelings overwhelm him once again. Furthermore, she was already with someone else. However, he braved his emotions, took the information, and went in search of Stacy.

Stacy had completed school at the top of her class and was in line to get a job at the same company Presley was employed. She wanted to reconnect with Presley and perhaps learn a little more about the company. She was being courted by several other companies, so she wanted to see which company would be the best fit for her. Presley's company was already in the forefront as Presley worked there. She also wanted to make sure her work-life balance would be suitable in the long run.

This reconnection was also a chance for her to reconnect with Presley, and a very good excuse, indeed. Perhaps, the very reason Presley did not catch on as the excuse for Stacy's outreach was just perfect. Stacy had broken up with her boyfriend from college. The differences were too great between the two, which created a rift that would never see a lasting relationship. Deep down, Stacy knew the challenges in her relationship were never due to differences between her ex-boyfriend and herself. That relationship was over the moment she started talking to Presley back in college. She thought nothing of it at the time. It was not until they parted ways, she realized a void was left in her life from Presley's departure. She realized she had fallen for him unknowingly but remained silent to not upset the balance of friendship. Though she was struggling with the emptiness that came from unfulfilled love, she managed to suppress it and focused on school. When Presley's company approached her, she knew that it was fate and was determined to once again, reconnect with the only man she had ever truly loved.

Lost in thought Stacy sat in her small, lonely studio apartment when a knock at the door broke her concentration.

"Who the heck is that?", she thought.

She carefully peeped through the door's spy glass to find a face that almost made her heart jump out of her chest.

"Presley!"...she exclaimed.

She opened the door and greeted Presley with the warmest of hugs and a very gentle, very long kiss on his cheek. Both were apologetic for their lack of communication over the last two years and vowed to do better. They continued talking for seemingly the whole night, reconnecting as they once did back in college, as if no time had passed. Presley still was not aware of the feelings Stacy had for him and was fully assured that they were still just friends; when she shared that she was being courted by his company and wanted to know more about the company before deciding. Presley had truly hoped there was more to her coming back into his life, but her request for information about the company shut down whatever hopes he had of something more than a friendship. He obliged her request and proceeded to let her know the ins and outs of his company; at least, the information to which he was privy. Then, maybe attempting to make a joke, a rush of blood, or something else, he decided to highlight the fact that the best thing about his company was that he was there. Stacy told him she was glad he said that because that was the main reason his company was at the top of her list. They both had a laugh and in one solemn moment as the two looked deeply into each other's eyes they both confessed their true feelings for one another. The moment led to confusion, surprise, and then delight. Finally, the two best friends, now one in heart, embraced and had the slowest, most tender kiss. A kiss filled with three years of pent-up, unbridled emotions finally confessed with unspoken tongues.

A fire was lit that night, one that would burn brightly

within the hearts of Presley and Stacy. No two had been more

in love. Presley was lucky to find a love rivaling only that of his

mother and father. His parents' love was an example of how

two people should love each other, and that example was

made evident in the way Presley loved Stacy. She, of course,

complemented him quite nicely with a love that was no less

than what she was receiving from Presley. Stacy decided to

accept the offer from Presley's company and soon thereafter

they moved in together. Now they were living and working

together, though not in the same department or building. They

loved and cherished every minute of life together. A year, then

two went by and Presley felt he could not wait a second more

to make Stacy his wife. So, he solicited the help of his aunt

and cousins to plan an engagement surprise for Stacy. He

wanted everything to be perfect, and he was not good at such

things. Give him an extremely complicated piece of equipment

and he could break it down and rebuild it within a matter of

minutes, but planning parties or events was always to be his

Achilles heel. His family agreed and after several weeks in

coordination with Presley they came up with a most

spectacular, romantic plan for the engagement. When this brilliant plan was finally executed, the answer was of course yes; at least when she stopped crying. The engagement period only lasted about three months as they were rather eager to be husband and wife. They got married on a beautiful spring day in a scene straight from a fairytale setting.

Another three years went by and the two were still deeply in love with one another. They traveled and enjoyed the time they had together. One day while home; just before bedtime, Stacy emerged from the bathroom with the biggest smile on her face. She announced in the sweetest voice possible.

"Honey we are Pregnant."

Presley, in shock, could only reply.

"Are you sure?"

Well, she was sure, and nine months later he had prepared and was ready to be a father. He had a great instructor in his own father and now it was time for him to do the same.

4 ANITA: NEW LIFE FROM YOUNG LOVE

The day of truth was finally upon the young couple. Stacy's water broke and little Anita was on her way. Stacy was immediately rushed to the hospital. On arrival the staff and doctor were ready and waiting for Stacy. Presley was given the option to be in the operating room, and he jumped at the chance. He would help to keep her calm during the birth. Everything started well but after a difficult stretch of labor, little Anita finally came out to see the new world. She was placed into the arms of mommy and both parents looked proudly at the new life they had made together. After a brief spell with the parents, baby Anita was taken by the nurse for a complete checkup. Then, in a short span thereafter, the doctors noticed a dramatic change in the vital signs of Stacy. She began to gasp for air and her eyes rolled over. The frightened Presley was quickly ushered out of the room, with the assurance that everything would be okay.

"Things like this happen from time to time"...the nurse stated.

As Presley waited in the waiting area, heart beating at a hundred miles per minute; all he could think about was how he would manage if anything was to happen to Stacy. How would he care for a baby girl all on his own? His family did the best they could to try to calm Presley. Just then the doctor walked out with the saddest most apologetic look on his face and Presley knew. He collapsed to his knees and was held up by his aunt, as best she could. Presley's whole world was once again brought crashing down around him. It was as if his heart was torn from his body. Part of him died that day along with Stacy. He felt guilty for getting her pregnant as if what happened was his fault. Presley had shut down again as he did when his parents passed. Nevertheless, his catatonic state did not last as long as it did when his parents died. He had something great to look forward to in his new baby girl. The thought of being there for her gave him the strength he needed to break free of his depression. His new goal in life was simple; to be the best provider and father he could be for this little girl. The things that were out of his realm, he would draft others to assist him.

Like anything that Presley tackled in life, fatherhood was no exception. He worked very hard and did what he said he would do for his daughter. He made sure to have the best care for Anita as a baby and had the support of his reliable aunt, Aunt Ena. He made sure he was there for Anita in the evenings and put her to bed every night. He tried to spend as much time with her as possible, even if it meant taking his work home. Most times he was very sad about the loss of Stac; especially when he gazed into Anita's little eyes, much like her mother's. Though this sadness lingered, it was something he had never once shown to Anita. The nights when the overwhelming feeling of gloom hit Presley, he retreated to his room where he would break down and cry for hours. Anita only saw a happy face when he was around her and he wanted to keep it that way. Over time the pain became less and less, and the joy for his daughter became stronger each day. The little things she did were enough to keep his spirits up and brought joy and laughter to his world again. Her laughter was the best remedy for a bad day. As the years passed by, Presley was resolute in the idea that his daughter and aunt would be the only women in his life.

It was already time for Anita to go to school, in what seemed like a flash for Presley. He did the research and asked around, but luckily the neighborhood in which Presley lived had a great school. He made all the preparations and got her enrolled. Though nervous, as it would be her first experience outside of the world, he had created. This was her first experience with other children besides her cousins. Presley knew it would be the best thing for her. Furthermore, he had already home-schooled Anita through to Pre-kindergarten, so now it was time for Presley to let her go. Although Presley was nervous, Anita seemed to have adapted well to her new environment, a trait from her mother. How she ended up being so brave did not matter to Presley, he was just excited and relieved that she was fine.

Presley did his best to give his little girl what she needed, including spending quality time with her. He tried not to spoil her, as he felt his parents might have done by over pampering him. Nevertheless, she was not born with the condition of social and behavioral awkwardness like Presley. He tried to be stern in disciplining Anita, but at times he would come off a bit rough. Imagine a man with the intelligence of a genius and the personality of a child raising a child, there were bound to be a few awkward moments. Presley knew when he was out of his depths and had his aunt to call upon when he needed help with Anita.

There was such a time. The day Anita got that special visit from nature, proclaiming that she was becoming a woman. Presley almost collapsed when Anita told him. He did not react to the news like a typical man would, turned off by the imagery of what is happening to the female body in that moment. No, instead he was in sheer shock. The thought that she just went from his innocent little baby girl to what could potentially become a reservoir of mixed-up, unbridled raw emotions all in one neat little package: a *teenager*. His little girl was quickly becoming a woman. To him, this meant soon, there would no longer be a need for him. Maybe if not altogether, then his role may be significantly reduced in her life. When Presley finally gathered himself, he made the call to his aunt, and she came right away. Luckily for him it was a Sunday, and his aunt was at home doing a little gardening in the backyard. When she received the call from Presley, she hurried over after making a brief stop for supplies suitable for the occasion. Upon arrival, Aunt Ena went into the bathroom with Anita and explained everything to her. She then allowed Anita to execute her instructions on her own. Aunt Ena then retreated outside the bathroom and locked arm in arm with Presley. Once outside, she broke it down for Presley and explained to him that this would be a very sensitive time for Anita so he should treat her with a cotton glove. She then went on to tell him the things he would need to keep in the house for the times when Anita gets her monthly period. She imparted her knowledge of the female biological processes unto poor Presley, and he was overwhelmed with all the information. After she imparted all her knowledge, she stopped and said,

"By the way. I don't know if you panicked or what, but this is unacceptable," holding up a mangled, tattered half roll of paper towel fashioned almost like a diaper.

"I had to cut this off of the poor girl, with all the tape you wrapped around it," explained Aunt Ena.

"You had it wrapped around her and taped up like she was ready to fight a sumo wrestler."

Presley looked at his aunt with a puzzled look on his face and said...

"Well, the commercial said it was super absorbent."

"I thought she was hurt and bleeding, before I realized what it was," he explained.

"I made it for her and after she put it on in privacy, I finished it up with some more tape."

"Unacceptable!" was once again uttered by Aunt Ena, shaking her head while giving Presley a wry smile.

He had his struggles, but overall Presley was a great

dad to Anita. As Anita got older, she got to the stage where she was more aware of her father's condition and how others treated him. She was very protective of him during her elementary school years, but something changed as she moved on to junior high school. She was under intense pressure to fit in, which meant that her relationship with her father suffered. She started to pull away more and more. She didn't want him to drop her to school anymore as she had become ashamed of him. She elected to take the school bus. Friends became more important to Anita than her father's feelings. She started to lose sight of who she really was; she began to go down a somewhat dark path. She became a person that no longer cared for the feelings of others, including her peers. She became one of the members of "the Society Crew" in her school. This group of young people from the elite and powerful families in the community was founded from the similar backgrounds they all shared. Even though Presley was not considered an elite member of the community, he gained notoriety from the work at his company. This allowed Anita a pass into the exclusive Society Crew. The students in this club were not particularly keen on being good. They were very disruptive to other students and the school in general. They felt they could do whatever they wanted and at times did just that. There was no real authority figure that would go against them as their parents "gave so much to the school." The free reign of the Society Crew continued from year to year, generation to generation, with no foreseen end in sight. Now Anita was a part of the very thing that her father fought against when he was in school. Presley never thought his daughter would end up being like those kids that bullied him so many years ago; not after the way he tried to raise her. Presley now had to face the same torment from his own daughter and in his own home. He tried his best to talk to her and steer her away from the bad influence of those society kids 'til he was at his wits end. He then once again brought in the big guns, Aunt Ena, who was up to the task. It took some time, but Aunt Ena finally broke through to Anita and got her away from the Society Crew. In fact, it wasn't until her last quarter of her sophomore year, when Anita broke away from the group. Anita's schoolwork immediately started to improve, her behavioral problems brought to a halt, and her involvement with other aspects of life at school improved. She eventually got involved with academic clubs in her school with the encouragement from of father. She also found some time to do something she liked to do. She loved to sing and act, so she joined the drama and theatre troupe at her school. Naturally, the kids from the Society Crew did not like that they were shunned by Anita and set out to make her life a living hell.

For a while life was very comfortable for Anita. However, that was short lived as the Society Crew decided to act. Now Anita felt what it was like to be on the receiving end of bullying. She did not like it one bit. She could not believe she made people feel the way she felt- angry, helpless, vulnerable, and emotionally scared. Whether it was her father's genes in her or maybe she had once again found her courage, she decided she had to fight back and fight back she did. She stood up to the head of the Society Crew, but she was in way over her head. The leader of the Society Crew loved the challenge and stepped up his aims to make Anita's life miserable. His tactics became more and more despicable. He obtained pictures of

Anita getting undressed while she was changing for her gym class and posted them on the school's website and other social media pages. Anita was furious and finally got Presley involved. This behavior had to stop, Presley thought, and immediately called his lawyer. The lawyer was able to make a case against the leader of the Society Crew along with several other members. The parents of all the kids from the Society Crew had their lawyers as well, but there was nothing they could have done to help them. The picture they had posted was of an under-aged minor. Armed with this information, Presley was able to strike a deal with all the parents of the kids involved and the school that would see an end to the reign Society Crew once and for all.

5 A STAR IS BORN

Newly emerged from her bout with the Society Crew, Anita was now a hero at her school. She was partly responsible for the demise of the dreaded scourge on the school and its students in the form of the Society Crew. She feared that she would still be ridiculed by the students at her school for the pictures taken of her, but she was met with surprising acceptance. No one cared about the pictures that were released, and they were now a distant memory. Her role in taking down the Society Crew gained her the respect of all her peers. Her life was again heading in the right direction. With the Society Crew obstacle behind her, she could once again focus on her studies and extra curricula activities.

Anita was doing well in school and her activities and

clubs were an important part of her life. Her dedication to the drama club and theatre was paying off as she became strong in her craft. Her voice greatly improved as she got older. By the time she was a senior she was the lead in all the musicals productions from her drama club. She became such an incredible singer that her other clubs asked her to host small concerts to raise money for them. These concerts became very popular within the community and even attracted people from outside of the community. They raised money not only for her clubs, but for the school as well.

One of the parents from the school invited a music executive friend, Jim Townsend, to one of her concerts. Anita's life would later take a dramatic turn, a life of stardom awaited. Jim approached Anita after her concert and presented her with an opportunity to come to his record company. Presley, of course, wanted her to finish school before she would be allowed to pursue a singing career. Jim and Anita both agreed to these terms; Anita had no choice really, as she was a minor and under the care of her father.

Jim was a self-made millionaire that worked his way up the ranks in the music industry. He earned the privilege of running the production company given to him by the company's owner when he retired from the business several years prior. Now Jim had made the company even more lucrative by moving the company into not only music production and management, but also television and movie production. Jim saw the future of the business and that was the very reason he saw the potential in Anita. She would fit in with the company easily due to her talents as a singer and an actress.

Upon the completion of school, Anita would be groomed by Jim's production company to be the next big star with plans that would see her on the big screen. The production company wanted to use her talents as an actress and a singer. Presley made sure that Anita understood the importance of having a back-up plan and insisted she took online college courses. Anita did not mind doing so, and felt it was important to have something to fall back on, if the music or acting did not work out.

Presley decided to support his daughter, so he took a leave of absence from his job to accompany her to Los Angeles for the first phase of Anita's music career. It was a sacrifice to put his job at risk. However, the respect Presley had earned from his company and its owner gave him peace of mind that he made the right decision. The owner called Presley to assure him that he thought what he was doing was admirable, and as a father himself, he understood. He also gave Presley the assurance that his job was secure and awaited his return, relieving any extra worries Presley had weighing on his shoulders. The father and daughter team packed up and flew out to Los Angeles. When they arrived in Los Angeles they were greeted with the royal treatment. Their baggage and transportation were all taken care of by the production company. They were accommodated in the best hotel. After a day of pampering, they were given a schedule for the next day and were told to have a good night's rest for the busy day ahead. After a good night's sleep and some great breakfast, the two were whisked away to a meeting with the production company and some of its staff members.

Jim introduced Presley and Anita to her new talent manager, Andy Brock. Brock was a go-getter; a fast-talking, smooth operator, and Presley did not like him. They said he was the best in the business and that he would be good for her career, so Presley had to just tolerate him. Brock was no slouch and picked upon Presley's disdain for him right away. He knew he had to get Anita away from daddy's influence as soon as he could to mold her into the image, he wanted her to be. So, he began his campaign of misguidance, lies, and manipulation. Anita was ill-equipped to deal with that at such a young age.

Brock saw something in Anita. Brock had been after Jim's job for a while, and by any means necessary he was going to get it. Somehow, he believed that Anita was the way to get the job at the head of the company. Brock was ruthless in his business dealings and an expert in negotiation tactics. These skill sets made him a lethal opponent. His first mission was to get daddy dearest out of the picture. He began filling Anita's head with lies and manipulated her to think her father was a bad image for her, all while trying to build her career. Anita loved her father but soon began to fall under the influence of Brock.

She then later went to her dad and asked him to return home under the guise that she was worried he might lose his job. Presley felt she was right and did not suspect that she was trying to get rid of him. He was starting to miss his work, and thought it was a better time than any to make the trip back home. He thought she was fitting in quite nicely with the production company and was well on her way to being a star. They spent the last couple days together before Presley was to return home. They did fun father-daughter activities, to spend as much time as possible together before he had to leave. The day Presley was scheduled to leave, Brock asked Presley to sign a few consent forms so Anita could travel. In the rush of it all, Presley did not see a paper Brock had slipped under the consent forms. It was a paper drafted up to relinquish parental rights and turn over legal guardianship of Anita to Brock. Evidently, Brock had put carbon paper between the two pieces of paper. When Presley thought he only signed for minor consent forms, but his signature was copied to the form below the carbon paper, giving up his parental rights to Anita.

Reluctantly, Presley boarded the plane, leaving the care of his only daughter in the hands of a man he barely knew. He took solace in the fact that the production company Anita was with was one of the nation's top companies at developing and managing young talent. Anita was happy for the opportunity she received, but she was worried about her father. Who would take care of him, she thought, and who would give her advice on what to do or not do?

Before she could finish her thought, Brock swooped in as if he could read her thoughts and proceeded to console her with his back-handed sentiment. His strategy was to keep her so busy she would not have time to think of her father, and it worked. When she was not in the studio, she was on photo shoots. When she was not doing photo shoots, she was at voice coaching sessions. When she was not at voice coaching sessions, she was at wardrobe fittings and shopping for clothes. When she wasn't doing all that, she was sleeping. She pretty much had no life outside of working for the production company, on her way to stardom. At first Presley and Anita were able to speak to each other consistently; even with Anita's busy schedule. Brock soon found out about their conversations and devised a plan to separate her from her father once and for all. He first started by denying calls to her room from her father; a deal he made with the night manager at the front desk of the hotel. When she inquired about her father, he then convinced her that her father did not need her anymore. He showed her the paperwork Presley signed giving all rights to Brock. Not knowing that it was a forgery, Anita was heartbroken and felt that her father had truly abandoned her. Brock had finally broken her to his will and now he could start on his next phase.

Everything was going according to plan. Subtle changes started to emerge in Anita. The more obvious changes were changes to her hair, make-up, and clothes; more specifically lack of clothes. She too was following in the trend of most starlets to wear less clothes to get more attention. Her behavior and mannerisms changed as well.

Under the tutelage of Brock, she became a self-absorbed diva and vanity hound, who was not very nice to the people around her. She was becoming a former version of herself when she was in high school, hanging with the Society Crew. Brock had firmly rooted himself in her life as a father figure, with the added advantage as somewhat a puppet master; pulling all her strings. Brock was going to use her, to ride her success all the way to the top. Now he was convinced, Jim would have no choice but to name him as his successor.

Indeed, it was amazing how quickly Anita grew in popularity. She worked hard on her first album and was seeing the rewards of her hard work in the reception she received from the public and the media. Everyone was surprised by her powerful and crisp voice; the pre-teens and teens quickly accepted her message of fun and young love. Her television personality and interview skills also boosted her acceptance, a direct benefit of Brock's coaching. Soon she was the number one pop star in America and was quickly gaining popularity around the world. Her concerts sold out in stadiums and arenas across the globe. Brock was already starting to see himself as the head of the company.

6 INSULT TO INJURY

Presley was so proud of what Anita had achieved and tracked her progress every step of the way. He was also told lies to as to why they could not communicate. They had not communicated for quite some time. Although he worried about her, he took solace in the fact that she was doing so well. She was everywhere, so it seemed as though she was still close by. He talked about her non-stop out of pride; always showing his co-workers and friends the newest thing she was doing. He talked about her to everyone and anyone in his everyday life. He was brimming with pride for his daughter. Presley could not help himself. My daughter is a worldwide pop star, he thought to himself.

However, the feeling of pride quickly became feelings of

concern. As her popularity grew, Anita's behavior was more erratic, and her dress became more scandalous. Presley began to get questions from his friends about her. Many wanted to know how he could allow her to dress that way and if he was comfortable with her looking the way she did? Presley had no answers. It was his daughter, but he felt powerless and withdrawn from her. He no longer had influence over her. As a father, he could not sit back and allow Anita to fall into this trap for the sake of fame. He decided to make the only move he could, which was to contact Jim.

"Jim, you promised me that my daughter would not be taken advantage of and made to look the way she does," explained Presley.

He voiced his concerns over how she was portrayed in the media and the mental strain it might be causing her. Presley demanded that Jim personally checked into her well-being and talk to those involved in creating her image. Jim immediately assured Presley he would do just that. As a father, he understood what Presley was going through. As a man of his word, he was going to uphold his promise to Presley and Anita.

The next day Jim called Brock into a meeting to get to the bottom of the Anita situation. Brock, however, thought the meeting was about something entirely different. He thought his big chance had finally come and Jim would name him the next CEO of the company. It took him completely by surprise when he found out the true nature of the meeting. He was berated because of how Anita became a success. Indeed, Jim and the company's shareholders were impressed with Anita's meteoric rise to stardom. However, Jim stated that it was against the company's belief system on how their artists are to be treated and portrayed in the public eye.

"Furthermore, I just got off the phone with Presley. He reminded me of the promise I made to him and Anita and it's a promise I intend to keep, so fix this."

Brock left that meeting steaming mad. He agreed to fix it, but he had no intention of fixing anything. His only thought was that Presley had interfered with his plans for the last time. He had to formulate a plan to get Presley out of Anita's life for good. It quickly came to him. Anita will be attending an award show next month at which she is receiving a new artist award.

"I will write her speech for her and in it she will refer to me as her father," he thought to himself.

His intention was to use the speech to destroy Presley, removing him from the equation and from future interactions with Anita.

The night of the award show had finally arrived, and Brock was ready. He armed Anita with an award acceptance speech that would surely be the undoing of Presley. Brock knew for sure Presley would not miss Anita's big night. He made certain of it by sending a letter to Presley on behalf of Anita to remind him to tune in. Presley knew about the award show and the award for which Anita was nominated. Weeks before the show he told everyone around him and all his friends from work to watch the award show at his house. So here it was the moment of truth. The main event was finally here. The host made the announcement,

"The award for best new artist goes to.... Anita."

As she walked onto the stage Brock smirked with a look of pure evil on his face.

"Go on read the speech and with a few words end the constant meddling from your inept daddy," he thought to himself.

Meanwhile, back at Presley's home, Presley beamed with joy and pride as his friends looked on.

"This is it everyone, Shhhh," Presley stated.

Anita stepped up to the microphone and started to deliver her speech, thanking everyone that had anything to do with her success, including her fans.

"Most of all I would like to thank the one person that made this all possible, without whom I would not be here today" Anita exclaimed.

Presley listened with a full heart, waiting for her to call his name. He was so proud of her and to hear her acknowledge his role in her life would be the greatest honor. However, she ended her speech with words that pierced

Presley's heart as if struck by a million tiny daggers.

"I would like to dedicate this award to my greatest asset, the man that is like a real father to me, my manager Brock."

While the end of her speech was met with thunderous applause at the award show, there was only silence at Presley's house. Presley stood silent, somewhat embarrassed, but in too much pain to even feel shocked. Presley was more sensitive to the situation due to his capacity to properly process the pain. Though it would have upset any parent in his position, it was more devastating to him. The pain he felt rivaled that of his parent's and Stacey's death. Seeing how Anita's speech profoundly affected Presley, one of his closest friends quietly said:

"Ok everyone let's go, let's give him some space. Are you going to be alright," he asked concerned.

A gesture met with silence and a wave of the hand by Presley, as if to wave him away. His friends all ushered out slowly, one by one they all exited the house. The door closing signaled a collapse to the knees by Presley and a tearful outburst. Presley was left wondering what he did wrong, why she hated him, and how she completely discarded him like that. He was truly heartbroken by her act of omission.

"Is she ashamed of me," he thought,

He felt she had completely disowned him as a father.

"Who would want me as a father anyway, especially someone as famous as her," he pondered, as he turned the blame on himself.

Presley replayed the scene over and over in his mind. Every time he remembered the part in Anita's speech when she called Brock's name, a new injury was to be inflicted on his heart. Even days after the award show, Presley was visibly shaken and heartbroken. He did not let it affect his work, but his personal relationships suffered. Presley was in a state of depression, and everyone noticed, despite all his efforts to put his best foot forward. Depression took hold and was there for the long-haul. Everyone was worried about Presley, but none more than his honorable aunt, Aunt Ena. She prayed for him to snap out of it and when she wasn't praying, she was talking with him.

Almost a year had passed since that faithful night and Presley was now at a point where he had to take some time from work. Presley spent most of this time outdoors at the parks. He felt at peace in the tranquil environment of the local parks. In those moments he could shut out the world and all the pain that it brought.

One cold wintery day as he sat still admiring the picturesque scene of the snow in the trees, he heard a faint sound down by the river. He went over to investigate, and much to his surprise found a scraggly little kitten struggling against the flow of the river to make it to the banks.

"How the heck did this kitten get there", he thought, as he immediately sprang into action.

Without thinking, he took his jacket off. He climbed down the slippery sloping bank of the river with jacket in hand, and jumped into the icy river, which was at about waist deep. He grabbed the kitten and immediately wrapped it up in his warm jacket. He made his way back up to the side of the river.

He placed the scared little kitten, now calm and cozy in the folds of his jacket, on the edge of the riverbank. He suddenly felt his left foot sliding backwards as he lifted his right leg to anchor himself on the edge of the river. He lost his balance and plunged into the freezing river once more. As he struggled to right himself, a swift current swept him under and smacked his head on a rock.

While all this was going on, a young couple taking a walk saw the whole thing. They were touched by his kindness to fish the poor little kitten out of the river. However, they were horrified to see the moment of triumph turn to disaster. The gentleman instructed his lady friend to call 911 and raced over to assist Presley. Presley's motionless body flowed with the current of the river downstream in a state of unconsciousness. The stranger pursued Presley frantically. He saw a point ahead where there was an overhanging branch directly above the water line. He raced ahead of Presley and fixed himself in a position on the branch that would make it easy to pull Presley from the river. By God's grace, the stranger was able to pull Presley to safety. Shortly thereafter, the paramedics arrived on the scene and the News teams followed suit. The reporters interviewed the stranger as a hero. After hearing him tell the story of what happened they also dubbed Presley as a hero. The story made its way to primetime news and quickly took off as a big story around the nation. The story was so popular that Presley's rescuer, whose name was Robbie, became a household name. Robbie went on a few nationwide daytime and late-night shows to tell the story. Each time he went he brought the little kitten Presley had saved. The story of the heroics of the two men tugged at the nation's heart strings. While on the press circuit, Robbie told the media that Presley, as he was later identified by the police, was still struggling for life in the hospital. When Presley was brought into the hospital, he was battling hyperthermia and had a bad head injury from hitting his head on a rock in the river. The head injury caused some swelling in his brain and the doctor's had to induce coma to help reduce the swelling. The story grew from there as now the watch was on to see if Presley would pull through his ordeal.

Across the country banners could be seen with the words -

Pray for Presley- written on them. The news media flocked to the hospital where Presley was being held under observations. Never have there been such a strong show of support for a common man, though he may have been considered a celebrity for his very heroic act. Flowers, balloons, and cards arrived at the hospital daily for Presley. The hospital had to dedicate a whole storage area for them.

A famous reporter was finally able to get permission from Presley's Aunt to speak with her. She thought she would introduce the world to who Presley was on a personal level via his aunt. The reporter was also granted access to Presley's room in the hospital. Aunt Ena knew this was an invasion on Presley's privacy, but she thought it was more important to allow everyone to get to know Presley. She felt this would allow a real connection with the man and the story. Some people had even begun to doubt the story of Robbie and thought he exaggerated the story to further his own agenda. On the contrary Robbie became closer to Presley the more he learned about him from his aunt and friends. They soon became inseparable, though Presley knew nothing of him. He spent countless hours with Presley, reading to him, holding his hand, and giving him words of encouragement.

Aunt Ena often visited Presley and followed a similar role as Robbie. Other friends from his job would come by as well, but none more dedicated than his boss and friend, Mr. Buxton. Mr. Buxton took time out from his busy schedule of running a top engineering firm to come see Presley as much as he could. That said a lot about Presley. Presley's boss took care of all of Presley's medical expenses, which were not covered by insurance.

While all this was happening, elsewhere Anita was preparing for an upcoming performance on tour. Brock knew what was going on with her father and he tried everything in his power to keep it from her. He used the excuse that it was to protect her. It was more like he was protecting himself or the money he was making from Anita. One day, however, during choreography practice, one of the dancers tuned into a trending story of two unlikely heroes: one left fighting for his life. Anita heard the name Presley and was instantly drawn over to watch along with the other ladies. The footage of the hospital room was shown in the news story. As if hit by a shot of electric current, a shockwave ran down the spine of Anita as she leapt to her feet from her kneeling position. Pointing to the screen of the girl's phone she shouted,

"That's my father."

"I thought Brock was your father", the girl replied.

In that one response, a year's worth of guilt, disgust, and anger instantly reared up in Anita as she lashed out bitterly.

"That horrible man is not my father, he is nothing to me, as a matter of fact, he is no longer my manager."

She gathered her belongings and stormed out leaving everyone mystified and shocked.

Anita immediately booked a ticket back home and left on the first flight out. Brock later went to the studio to check up on things and found out that Anita had left. He knew she could only be going to one place and was going to stop at nothing to bring her back. Jim, the head of the company got wind of

Brock's intentions and blocked him when he attempted to request the company private jet. He also cancelled Brock's corporate credit card. Jim was never a big fan of Brock, but he cared very much for Anita and respected Presley.

As Anita traveled to see her father, the guilt kept eating away at her little by little. Her emotions were all over the place and it was evident in her appearance. She did not know the story was a week old and that her father made a full recovery. Two days earlier the swelling on his brain had gone down. Presley woke up from his coma surrounded by his family, friends, and a strange little man he had never seen before holding his hand.

"Welcome back Presley, my name is Robbie, we will catch up later, for now it is good to see you finally up," Robbie excitedly told Presley.

His aunt and friends all greeted Presley with a big hug, thanking God that he was back. Presley was touched by the sincere gesture of everyone. He inquired about his current state and how he got there in the first place. Robbie was ready and very happy to explain everything. The happy news quickly spread throughout the hospital and of course to the news outlets. Everyone was abuzz as the news spread throughout the nation. Everyone rejoiced and for one moment in time people were able to celebrate something good in the world, instead of the usual doom and gloom happening around them. Two days later the famous reporter returned to finish the story of the two heroes with an interview right there in Presley's hospital room. Since the room was shared by another male patient in coma, they pulled the large curtain divider to respect the man's privacy. Presley's roommate was closer to the room's entrance while Presley was further inside the room. As the reporter began the interview with the two men, Robbie surprised Presley with the kitten he had kept hidden in the corner of the room.

"Remember this little guy," Robbie exclaimed,

pulling a sleepy little kitten out of the box. As if day turned to night, Presley's eyes went pitch black at the sight of the kitten. Presley did not come back from the coma alone. Something dark and very sinister returned with him and had now taken over his consciousness. He crushed the kitten in the palms of his hands as if he was crumpling foil paper. Blood oozed out of every orifice, as everyone froze in shock. Presley grabbed the neck of Robbie and snapped it with the ease of breaking a strand of dried uncooked spaghetti. Still frozen in shock, the reporter let out the most blood curdling scream one could imagine as Presley ripped the camera from the camera man and bludgeoned him to death with it. He then turned the camera to the lady reporter.

"You are now live on camera", he stated.

He proceeded to ram the camera through her frail frame, instantly and permanently silencing her deafening scream.

"Excuse me, Mr. Goodson, you're on air," whispered a soft female voice.

"Oh, I am sorry," replied Presley, "you caught me in a very weird and dark daydream or should I say day mare."

Presley somehow drifted off into a disturbing vision and a

game of the 'worse possible scenario outcomes for the interview.' The elaborate scene was a very realistic encroachment of a vivid dark conjuring of his imagination. On the contrary, he was summoned back to the present realm of his true consciousness. He realized that the comfortable little kitten had fallen asleep in his hands; purring away, as the news camera rolled on. He looked down at the innocent little creature, so small and fragile. He thought to himself how this little thing could survive such an ordeal. Presley's eyes were full of tears as he cuddled the little kitten close to his bosom. The entire experience came rushing back to him; a reminder of the value of life and how quickly we can lose it.

"You caused all this trouble, little troublemaker, and I would gladly do it again," stated Presley in his typical slow natured speech.

The entire country was watching the live interview and became even more touched by Presley. He was not the greatest of speakers, but somehow people were more drawn to him for that very same reason. He came across as very genuine and that was rare to find nowadays. The interview went on and everything was going well, when a strange emotional outburst interrupted the live broadcast. It seems a young lady, tears streaming down her face and sobbing endlessly, had entered the room on the other side of the hospital room curtains. The young woman could not control herself as she looked at the bandaged lifeless figure, with all kinds of tubes protruding from his arms and neck, and ventilator breathing for him. The suction sound of the ventilator and all the other monitoring devices in the room made the young lady even more uneasy, but did not deter her from her business at hand. As the news crew, the reporter, and the two heroes looked on through various gaps in the separating curtain, the young lady began to bare her soul to the unconscious man lying on that confounded bed. She apologized for being a difficult child; she apologized for the way she has acted over the past 2 years. She began to cry even more when she apologized for completely disowning him on national television. Presley could not stand it anymore, for as much as he liked hearing his daughter's apology, it hurt him very much to see her this way.

He jumped from behind the curtain shouting that he forgives her for everything and was happy to see her there at the hospital. The startled, surprised, and somewhat confused Anita was more than anything else happy to see that her father was alive and well.

"I thought that...." Anita started before Presley interrupted.

"I know you did," he said, "but I could not stand to see you cry anymore."

That was me a couple of days ago, but I am back and this time I am not letting you go again. The reporter could not believe what she was seeing. She signaled to the camera man at the other end of the curtain to start filming; to which he replied that he never stopped. The reporter could not believe that this simple little guy, who was now a national hero, also happened to be the father of the hottest, most exclusive pop star in the world. She was not going to miss this opportunity and the feel-good story of the century.

As the two embraced, enjoying the moment and giving thanks for having each other, the pale menacing figure of

Brock came sauntering into the room.

"Well, isn't this cozy," he blurted out.

His voice enraged Presley as he grabbed his daughter and shielded her behind him, acting as a barrier between Brock and his daughter.

"You are not a very nice man, stated Presley, "and I don't want you around my daughter anymore."

Brock told him his daughter had no choice; she was under contract with the company, and she had to come back with him. Brock also told Presley that he had already signed guardianship of Anita over to him. Presley did not recall signing anything like that and told him the only thing he signed was the consent forms for her to travel. Anita was not surprised to hear this as she always had doubts that her father would just abandon her. However, at the time she was very vulnerable and fragile, and Brock took advantage of her state.

"Okay, okay you got me; I tricked you into signing over guardianship, but who is going to believe you, a loser half-wit of a father."

Suddenly, out of the blue, as if something had snapped in her, Anita hit Brock in the face with a martial arts move rivaling that of Bruce Lee. Brock fell to the floor grabbing his nose as blood came gushing out.

"You broke my nose," he shouted, screaming and crying like a little kid who lost his toy. "No one talks about my father like that," Anita exclaimed.

The reporter saw this as a great time to make her presence known so she slid the separating curtain back to reveal herself, her camera man, and Robbie. Anita looked at Presley and asked if they were there the whole time, to which Presley replied,

"Yes, I am sorry they were here to interview me."

Anita was ecstatic, "this may be greatest news ever," she explained.

She asked the reporter if she recorded everything, and the reporter's answer was indeed yes. Presley didn't understand why that was important. Anita explained that it meant they also recorded Brock's confession of tricking him into signing away his parental rights. Since the broadcast was live, the executives and the board at Brock's company saw it and fired him. He was also immediately arrested for fraud by the cops already onsite at the hospital.

Presley and Anita both took solace in the moment, and once again embraced each other. Tears filled both their eyes as the nation looked on, enthralled and touched by this beautiful moment.